Charles Toscano

MATTHEW 21 : 22

ZONDERKIDZ

Papa's Pastries
Copyright © 2010 by Charles Toscano
Illustrations © 2010 by Sonja Lamut

Requests for information should be addressed to:

Zonderkidz, *Grand Rapids, Michigan 49530*

Library of Congress Cataloging-in-Publication Data

Toscano, Charles.
  Papa's Pastries / by Charles Toscano ; [illustrated by Sonja Lamut].
      p. cm.
  Summary: Miguel sees the results of his father's faith and generosity
when, although his own family is facing the oncoming winter with threadbare
clothing, a leaky roof, and no firewood, Papa gives away the pastries he has
baked.
  ISBN-13: 978-0-310-71602-0 (hardcover)
  [1. Christian Life—Fiction. 2. Poverty—Fiction. 3. Faith—Fiction.
4. Generosity—Fiction.]   I. Lamut, Sonja, ill. II. Title.
  PZ7.T645743Pap 2010

[E]—dc22   2008048897

Editor: Barbara Herndon
Art direction: Jody Langley

Printed in China

10 11 12 13 14 15 /LPC/ 6 5 4 3 2 1

Papa's Pastries

written by Charles Toscano
illustrated by Sonja Lamut

ZONDER**kidz**

ZONDERVAN.com/
AUTHORTRACKER
follow your favorite authors

Miguel awoke before dawn.

Kerplink...
    Kerplink...
        Kerplink...

Raindrops dripped through a hole in the roof. They dropped—one after another after another— into Mama's clay pot set in the middle of the dirt floor. The rooftop was as leaky as an old, wooden bucket.

Brrrrrrr... Miguel dressed quickly. His clothes were paper-thin and worn. They provided little warmth on this cold morning.

Papa was already awake. He was baking pastries for today's journey. The fire was nearly out, and the once-towering stack of firewood was now nothing more than twigs and sawdust. Without firewood there would be no fire; without fire there would be no pastries; and without pastries to sell, Papa could earn no money.

Miguel watched from the shadows as Papa knelt beside the fire and humbly bowed his head.

"Dear Lord, winter is drawing near, and my family needs many things. Without a new roof, firewood, and clothing, we will not survive. Please bless this day, Lord, that it may be a prosperous one. Be with us. Amen."

Papa rose and removed the pastries from the oven. Miguel hurried to his side. *Don't worry, Papa,* Miguel thought to himself. *Today, we will sell many pastries!* Together they filled a large sack with the tasty treats and began their journey to three nearby villages.

As Miguel and Papa entered the first village, Papa began to sing. He was known throughout the land for his wonderful pastries, but loved all the more for his beautiful voice.

The villagers sang! They danced! They clapped and cheered!

Miguel's heart filled with hope. *Surely*, he thought, *we will sell many, many pastries here!*

But alas, the villagers said to Papa, "We are sorry, señor, but we have faced many hardships, and money is scarce. We cannot afford to buy your delicious pastries."

Miguel's heart sank.

He watched as Papa shook hands with one of the villagers. Señor Gonzalez
was as thin as a skeleton.

Papa removed several pastries from the sack and gave them to the man.

"Gracias, mi amigo!" Señor Gonzalez cried. "Thank you, my friend!" The two men shook hands again, and Papa and Miguel continued on their journey.

When Miguel and Papa entered the second village, townsfolk flooded the square. They too enjoyed Papa's delightful songs. They too sang and danced and clapped and cheered!

Once again, Miguel's heart filled with hope. *Here we will surely sell many pastries!* he thought.

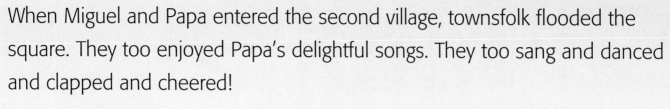

But alas, here too the villagers said, "We are sorry, señor, but we have faced many hardships, and money is scarce. We cannot afford to buy your delicious pastries."

Miguel's heart deflated.

He watched as Papa greeted Señor Vega with his wife and baby. Miguel noticed that their feet were bare and dirty, just like his own; their clothes were ragged and worn thin, just like his own.

Papa removed several pastries from the sack and offered them to Señor Vega.

"Gracias, mi amigo!" Señor Vega hugged Papa tightly. "Thank you, my friend!"

The two men shook hands, and Papa and Miguel continued on their journey.

When they entered the third village, townsfolk crowded the square. The villagers here too enjoyed Papa's songs. They too sang and danced! They too clapped and cheered!

But alas, they too said, "We are sorry, señor, but we have faced many hardships, and money is scarce. We cannot afford to buy your delicious pastries."

Miguel's heart broke.

Papa had sold no pastries and the sun was setting. It was time to return home.

Outside their own village, Miguel and Papa came upon a tiny hut. It was old and crumbling and barely standing. Papa waved to the elderly woman standing in the doorway.

Señora Santana welcomed them cheerfully. "Hola, muchachos!" she called. "Hello, boys!" She hurried inside and returned with a pitcher of tea.

Miguel and Papa sat for a short while. They rested their tired legs and enjoyed the sweet, savory tea. Papa removed the remaining pastries from the sack and handed them to Señora Santana.

"Gracias, mi amigo!" Señora Santana hugged Papa warmly. "Thank you, my friend!"

Then Papa and Miguel journeyed home, empty-handed.

When they arrived, Mama asked anxiously, "Papa, did you sell many pastries?"

"No," he said sadly. "I sold none."

"Then where are all of the pastries, Papa?" asked Miguel's brothers and sisters, peeking into the empty sack.

"I gave them away," he smiled tenderly, "to friends and families needier than our own."

Mama threw her hands into the air. She cried, "Now we have nothing! You are very kind, Papa, but very foolish. Kindness won't fix our leaky roof, nor fuel our fire, nor mend our worn clothing."

"Kindness is far more valuable than money," Papa replied. "The more you give away, the more you shall receive." And he yawned and stretched and set off for bed.

Later Miguel climbed onto his bed, tired and confused. He took a long, last look at the hole in the roof. What will tomorrow bring? There was no firewood, and now there were no pastries. *What will happen to my family?* Miguel thought as he rolled over and drifted off to sleep.

The next morning, Miguel awoke to heavy hammering on the housetop. Señor Gonzalez had come to visit. "I am a carpenter," he said, "and I have come to repay your kindness."

At noon, Miguel heard chopping in the woods. Señor Vega had come to visit.
"I am a woodcutter," he said, "and I have come to repay your kindness."

After noon, Miguel heard voices in the kitchen. Señora Santana had come to visit.

"I am a seamstress," she said, "and I have come to repay your kindness."

That evening, Miguel knelt beside the roaring fire and humbly bowed his head.

"Dear Lord," Miguel whispered, "thank you for your many blessings. Thank you for your loving kindness. And thank you, Lord, for my Papa. Amen."

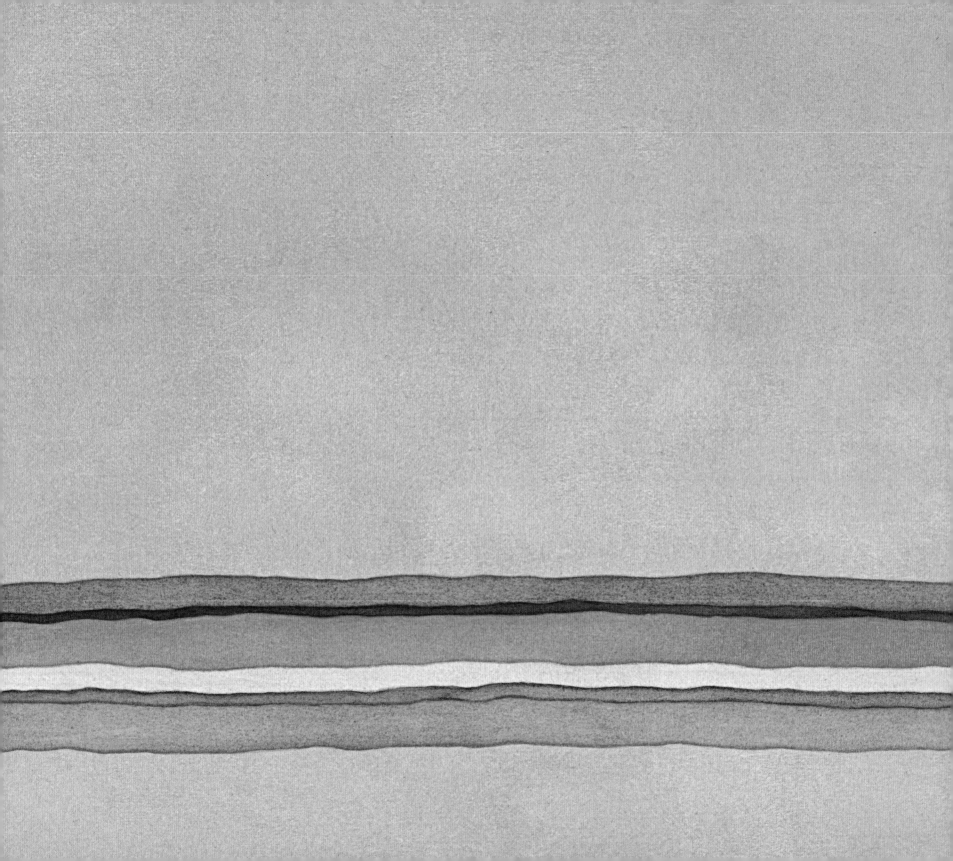